For my dad

Copyright © 2014 by Jamie Harper

First edition 2014

Library of Congress Catalog Card Number 2012950558
ISBN 978-0-7636-5562-4

CCP 19 18 17 16 15 14
10 9 8 7 6 5 4 3 2 1

Printed in Shenzhen, Guangdong, China

This book was typeset in Agenda.
The illustrations were done in block prints and mixed media collage,
using watercolor, ink, and cut paper.

Candlewick Press
99 Dover Street
Somerville, Massachusetts 02144

visit us at www.candlewick.com

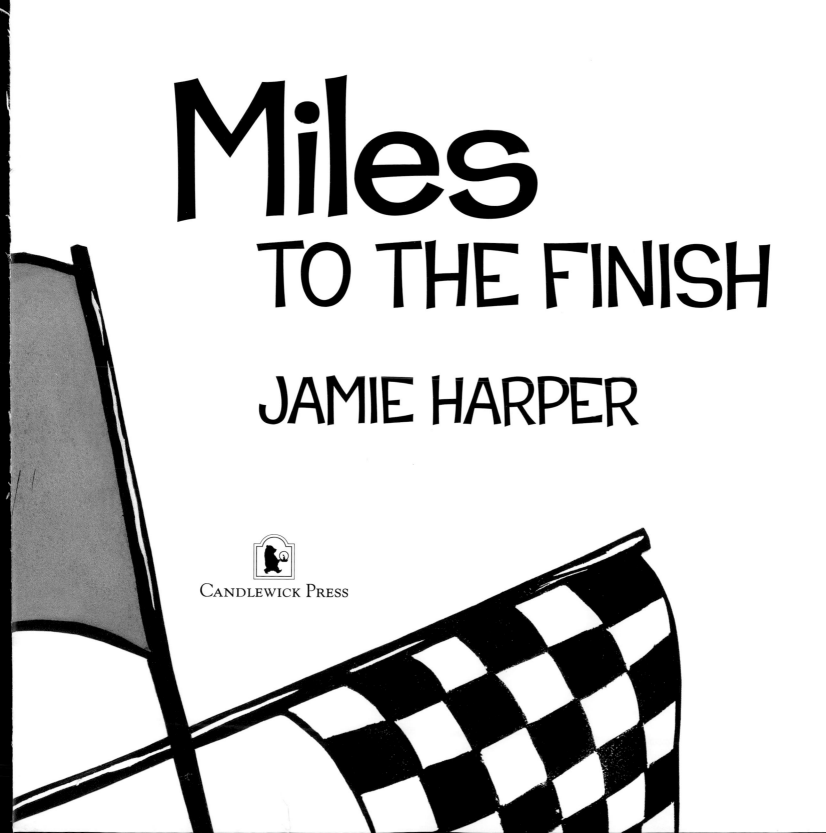

Miles
TO THE FINISH

JAMIE HARPER

CANDLEWICK PRESS

"Check it out —
it's a Speedster 660!"
says Otto.

"Where did it
come from?"
asks Miles.

"That's my car. I'm Indie.
  Are you racing today, too?"

"How fast does it go?" asks Miles.

"Fast," says Indie.

Miles has to be in tip-top shape
if he's going to beat the Speedster.

At recess, he gets a full tune-up.

He runs.

He climbs.

He does some heavy lifting.

His car gets a new look.

Miles is ready for the race.

The cars line up. The drivers wish one another good luck.

"Cool stickers!" says Indie.

Vroom, vroom, vroom goes the Speedster.

TAP, TAP, TAP go Miles's feet.

apple school grand prix

"Hey, make room for Axel," says Jane.

"START YOUR ENGINES!" shouts the flagman.

Miles takes the lead early.

Watch out! Rough track ahead!

Screeeeech! Miles escapes
the three-car pileup.

CRUNCH!

Here comes Indie.
Miles moves his
feet faster.
Oh, no! Otto spins
out at the turn.
Axel is still
hanging on.

ERRRRRH!

Miles stops and backs up.

"Otto, you okay?" calls Miles.

"Go, go, go!" yells Otto.

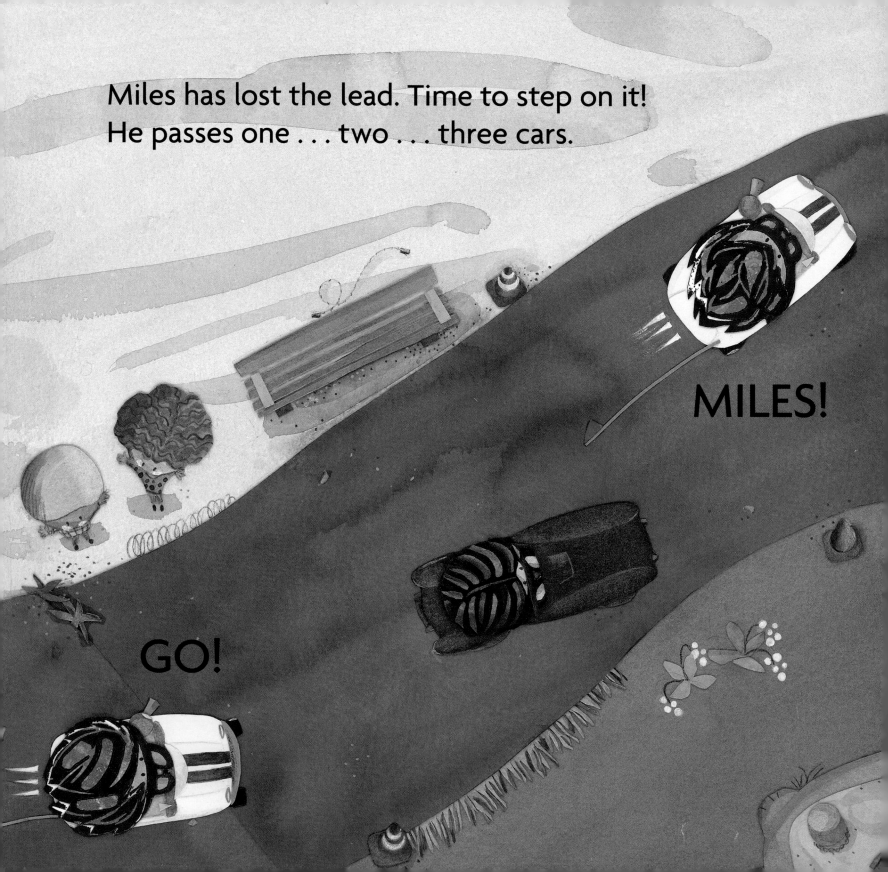

Miles has lost the lead. Time to step on it!
He passes one . . . two . . . three cars.

MILES!

GO!

GO!

Miles and Indie are side by side.

This is my chance, thinks Miles.
I can win!

Then Miles slows down and
thinks some more.

"Get in!" he hollers.

Miles speeds up. But Axel zooms by and crosses the finish line in first place.

The crowd roars.
"HOORAY!"

"YAHOO!"

The class celebrates
the victory.

Miles will, too. But not until he and Indie get the Speedster running again.